T0197692

The Adventures of the Great One

C. L. Wade

ISBN: Softcover 978-1-5035-2459-0
EBook 978-1-5035-2458-3

Rev. date: 12/18/2014

To order additional copies of this book, contact:
Xlibris
1-888-795-4274
www.Xlibris.com
Orders@Xlibris.com

The Adventures of the Great One

C. L. Wade

SCHOOL BUS

Every school day morning my dad starts the day with me. He tells me how great I am. He says, "son you can be whatever you want to be, all you have to do is work hard everyday in school." He calls me The Great One and tells me that I can be as great as my mind can imagine. Daddy says everyone is not going to be friendly, and to just ignore those that try to mistreat you. My parents always teach me to treat people how I would want to be treated.

HA-HA HA

One day after I got on the school bus , some of the kids laughed at me because they thought my new hair cut looked funny. I just ignored them like my dad told me to do. Besides, my Uncle Jamal cut it for me; he calls it a mohawk, and said that it was the latest hairstyle for boys. I'm the the only kid that looks like me that rides on my bus.

I am the only Kindergartner in my class that can read and write. My teacher always asks me to read out loud in front of the class. Mom and Dad taught me how to read and count before I was two. They said you can do anything that you put your mind to. Some of the white kids still laugh at my hair, and the black kids say that I sound white. I just ignore them like mom and dad tell me to.

My teacher says that she loves my new hair cut and to ignore them if they laugh. She said, "you're the smartest kid in my class when it comes to science and math."

When I am at school, my little brother and sister patiently wait. They love me just as I am and think everything I do is great. I teach them everything that I learn. When they start school they'll already know more than most kids in their class.

LUNCH

Before I could make friends with them they beat me to the punch. They even tried to bully me while eating lunch. But I just ignored them. I just read the books that my dad gave me about math and science. Before I knew it, I made friends with other kids who were equally interested in learning.

On my way home riding the bus, I did my homework or read a book without a fuss. When I got off the bus who did I see, my daddy and little sister waiting on me. My sister would run to me and give a big hug. Nothing else mattered because I knew I was loved.

Daddy said," it takes hard work to get what's rightfully yours. The homework they are giving you is too easy," so he challenged me some more. He gave me more to read before I could play video games or go outdoors.

Bedtime stories were my favorite. Dad would read a book making it so interesting. After he read to me, my imagination took me on journeys far beyond my bedroom.

HARVARD
UNIV.
Geophysics

Along the way my family was always there for me. My daddy lead our family with love and compassion, and never gave up on me. He taught me that the world is yours and to ignore those that have negative tendencies. Many of those lessons I still draw from today. I dedicate my doctorate degree in Geophysics to my family. I love them so much.